SomeONE

A Story of Acceptance
written by Jay & Bodie Ostrowski

Arcade Publishing
New York

Arcade Publishing books may be purchased in bulk at special discounts for sales promotion, corporate gifts, fund-raising, or educational purposes. Special editions can also be created to specifications. For details, contact the Special Sales Department, Arcade Publishing, 307 West 36th Street, 11th Floor, New York, NY 10018 or info@skyhorsepublishing.com.

Arcade Publishing® is a registered trademark of Skyhorse Publishing, Inc.®, a Delaware corporation.

Visit our website at www.skyponypress.com.
Visit the authors' website at www.someonethebook.com

10 9 8 7 6 5 4 3 2 1

Manufactured in China, May 2018
This product conforms to CPSIA 2008

Library of Congress Cataloging-in-Publication Data is available on file.

Cover design by Brian Peterson
Cover illustration by Jay and Bodie Ostrowski

Print ISBN: 978-1-62872-969-6
Ebook ISBN: 978-1-62872-970-2

Dedicated to someone . . . you know who you are

One day at recess, Someone wanted to play.

Everybody told him that Anybody would play,
but Someone only wanted to play with Somebody.

"Why not Anybody?" asked Everybody.
"Because he's just Anybody," answered Someone.

"And look, he's playing with Nobody."
"What's wrong with Nobody?" asked Everybody.
"None of us want to play with Nobody," answered Someone.

So he waited for Somebody...

and he waited. . . and he waited. . . and he waited.

He watched as Anybody played with Everybody.

He watched as Everyone played with Anyone.

Then he saw Somebody join in the game with Anybody and Nobody. They all seemed to be having a great time.

When the bell rang and recess was over,
Someone asked Somebody,
"Why would you play with Anybody and Nobody?"

Somebody answered,"I don't know, I like to play with Anybody, and Nobody asked me to."

That night, Someone thought about what Somebody said.

The next day, Someone didn't care who he played with.
He played with Anyone, Anybody, Everybody, Everyone,
Somebody, and Nobody.

It didn't matter. And they all had fun.

The End.